P9-EDK-187

ONE SEAL

by John Stadler

Orchard Books
New York

Orchard Books, A Grolier Company
95 Madison Avenue, New York, NY 10016

Manufactured in the United States of America
Printed and bound by Phoenix Color Corp.
Book design by Mina Greenstein
The text of this book is set in 24 point Gloucester Old Style MT.
The illustrations are watercolor.

10 9 8 7 6 5 4 3 2 1

Library of Congress Cataloging-in-Publication Data
Stadler, John.
One seal / by John Stadler.
    p.   cm.
Summary: A boy runs after his kite down to the beach and
meets an amazing assortment of animals who help him get his kite
back—temporarily.
ISBN 0-531-30195-8 (trade : alk. paper).
ISBN 0-531-33195-4 (lib. bdg. : alk. paper)
[l. Animals—Fiction. 2. Cooperativeness—Fiction.
3. Beaches—Fiction.] I. Title.
PZ7.S77575Op 1999 [E]—dc21 99-11664

For you

A child ran alone among the dunes.

A sudden gust of wind snatched the kite from his hands.

He ran after it.

He followed it down to the beach.
And that is where he saw the seal.

One seal.

And that is where the whole thing started.

One . . .

. . . by one . . .

. . . they came.

All of them.

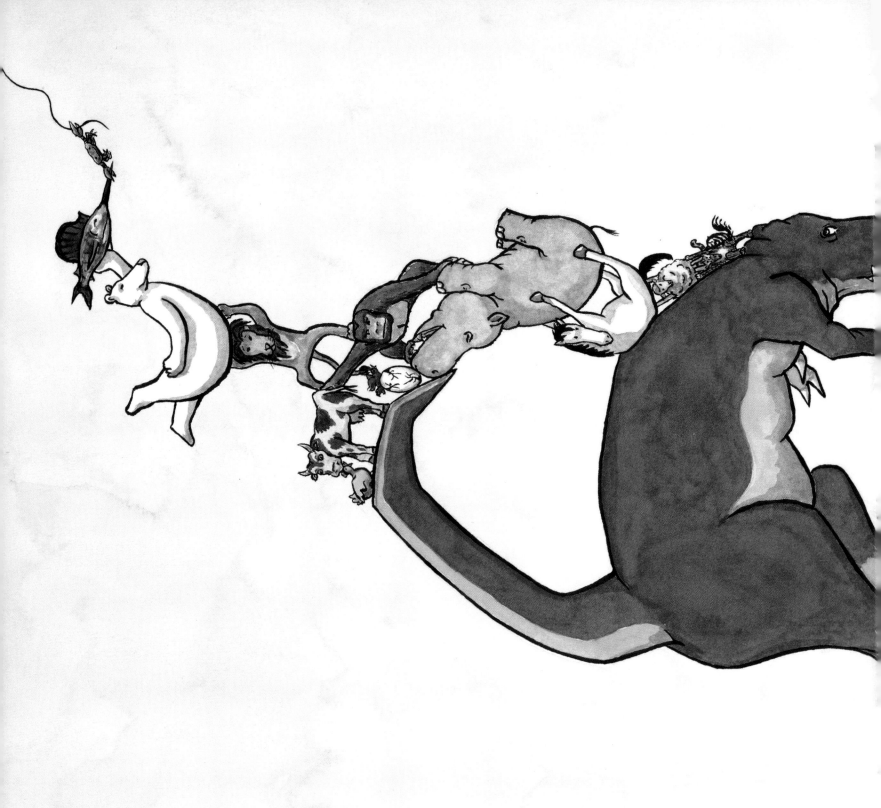

Photographs were taken.

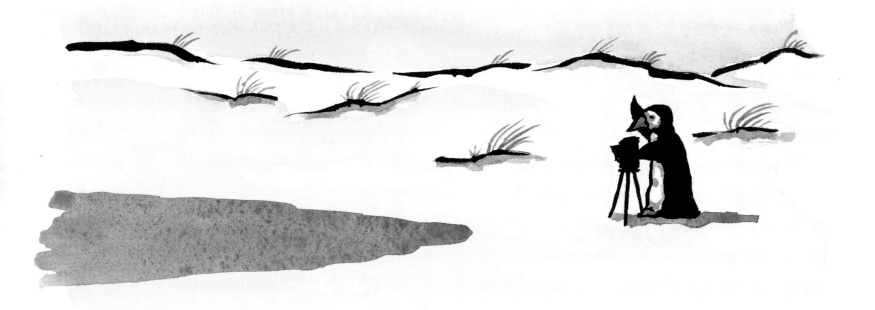

Names, addresses, and phone numbers were exchanged.
All agreed that they must get together soon and
do it again.

Then, slowly . . .

. . . one . . .

. . . by one . . .

. . . they left.

All of them.

Except for one.
One seal.

And then only the child remained.

Oops!